UNM-GALLUP
ZOLLINGER LIBRARY
200 COLLEGE ROAD
GALLUP, NEW MEXICO 87301

1. Books may be checked out for 28 days with no renewals.

2. A fine is charged for each day a book is not returned according to the above rule. No book will be issued to any person incurring such a fine until it has been paid.

3. All injuries to books beyond reasonable wear and all losses shall be made good to the satisfaction of the Librarian.

4. Each borrower is held responsible for all books charged on his card and for all fines accruing on the same.

GAYLORD R

MOUNTAIN
ANIMALS
IN DANGER

SURVIVORS SERIES · FOR CHILDREN

MOUNTAIN
ANIMALS
IN DANGER

by

Gary Turbak

illustrated by

Lawrence Ormsby

Northland Publishing

The artist would like to thank the following biologists and photographers for help in providing research to illustrate the animals in this book: George Andrejko, Arizona Game and Fish Department (Hualapai Mexican vole); Allan Carey (mountain lions and grizzly bear); Tim Haugen (gray wolf); Dave C. Hudson (California condor); Robert Mesta, U. S. Fish and Wildlife Service (California condor); Middleton/Liittschwager (northern spotted owl); Bob Miles, Arizona Game and Fish Department (Mount Graham red squirrel); Tom Stack and Associates (spotted owl); Dale Steele (Point Arena mountain beaver); Tom Ulrich (woodland caribou); and Michael Wallace, Los Angeles Zoo (California condor).

First Edition

ISBN 0-87358-573-9
Library of Congress Catalog Card Number 94-26302

Cataloging-in-Publication Data
Turbak, Gary.
Mountain animals in danger / by Gary Turbak ; illustrated by Lawrence Ormsby.
p.   cm. — (Survivors series for children)
ISBN 0-87358-573-9 : $14.95
1. Mountain fauna—Juvenile literature.   2. Endangered species—Juvenile literature.
[1. Mountain animals.   2. Endangered species.]
I. Ormsby, Lawrence, 1946- ill.   II. Title.   III. Series.
QL113.T97   1994   94-26302
599.052'9—dc20

Designed by Carole Thickstun
Edited by Erin Murphy and Kathryn Wilder
Production by Rudy J. Ramos
Production supervised by Lisa Brownfield
Manufactured in Hong Kong by Wing King Tong

0461/5M/10-94

To Peter Curley, who—like the animals in this book—has had to fight for life.

—G. T.

In memory of Betti Albrecht (1957–1993), who conceived these books out of love and caring for her daughter, Amy Rose; and to Amy Rose, that she might read them knowing that.

—L. O.

Pteranodons died about sixty-five million years ago, when all dinosaurs became extinct. They measured about twenty-five feet (the size of four beds laid end to end) from wingtip to wingtip.

J. Lofaro '84

What It Means to Be Endangered

This book is about animals living in the mountains—
but not just any animals. The animals in this book
are endangered. This means there aren't very many
of them. They are in danger of becoming extinct.
"Extinct" means the last animal of that kind has died.

Many animals have become extinct. Dinosaurs are
extinct. Dodo birds are extinct. Woolly mammoths are
extinct. You will never see one of those animals alive.
The animals in this book could become extinct, too.

Why Are These Animals Endangered?

Mountain animals become endangered for many reasons. Sometimes their habitat disappears. The place where they live is called their habitat. Mountain habitat can disappear when people cut down too many trees. This is how woodland caribou and northern spotted owls became endangered. Habitat also can be lost when people build too many roads or houses in the mountains where animals live. This happened to the Point Arena mountain beaver.

Wild animals also become endangered when people persecute (pronounced *PER-si-cute*) them. This means they kill the animals on purpose. People used to shoot and poison wolves, grizzly bears, cougars, condors, and bald eagles. Today, it's against the law to harm an endangered animal.

Sometimes, people kill animals by accident. When farmers spray pesticides (pronounced *PES-ti-sides*) on their crops to kill bugs, fish can eat poisoned bugs and get sick, too. If bald eagles eat those fish, they can get sick and lay eggs with thin shells. This makes the babies inside the eggs die. The farmers have poisoned the eagles by accident.

Some mountain animals become endangered because they are isolated. This means no other animals like them live nearby. Mount Graham red squirrels and Hualapai Mexican voles are isolated. There is only one small group of each.

What Kinds of Animals Are These?

This book features ten endangered mountain animals. Three are birds. Birds fly and lay eggs, but some other animals do those things, too. Birds, however, are the only animals that have feathers.

The rest of the animals in this book are mammals. Mammals have live babies. They don't lay eggs like birds. Mammals also feed milk to their babies and usually have fur or hair. People are mammals, but people certainly aren't endangered.

The ten animals in this book aren't the only endangered ones in the mountains. There are lots of others.

Gray Wolf

Gray wolves live in packs. The strongest wolf,
called the alpha male or alpha female, is the
leader. Wolves hunt deer, elk, and other

Not all gray wolves are gray. Wolf fur can be white, black, or many shades of gray or brown.

wild animals. When wolves make a kill, they usually eat every part of that animal, including many bones. Sometimes, wolves also kill cows and sheep. This is why some people hate wolves. Many people also believe that wolves like to attack humans, but this isn't true. Wolves are really afraid of people.

This nose can smell prey—like a moose or a deer—more than a mile away

In the spring, one female wolf in the pack has about five babies, which are born in a burrow. Wolf babies look a lot like puppies.

Wolves are endangered because people have killed too many of them.

This is the actual size of a wolf track.

Mount Graham Red Squirrel

This red squirrel lives only on one Arizona mountain—Mount Graham. The mountain is surrounded by desert, and biologists (people who study animals) call it a "sky island." Because the mountain is a kind of island, no new squirrels can come to Mount Graham.

During the summer, Mount Graham red squirrels collect hundreds of pine cones and store them in a huge pile on the ground. During the winter, they eat seeds from these cones. Each day, a squirrel eats the seeds from more than a hundred cones.

Mount Graham red squirrels are endangered because they are so isolated (far away from other squirrels). Also, some of their habitat has been lost.

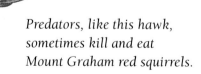

Predators, like this hawk, sometimes kill and eat Mount Graham red squirrels.

A bushy tail keeps the squirrel warm when the weather gets cold.

Sharp claws help make the squirrel an expert climber.

Some squirrels dig nest holes in old trees like this.

Cougars are the
largest wild cats
in North America.
Some weigh as
much as a man.

Eastern Cougar

This big cat is like a ghost. The western mountains of America have lots of cougars, but few—if any—live in the eastern United States. Some people say they have seen cougars in the East, but biologists aren't sure these cats still live there.

Cougars are also called mountain lions and pumas. They are skilled predators. (A predator is

Deer are the cougar's favorite food.

The cougar's strong jaws can bite through the neck of a deer. Its keen eyes and ears help it find food.

There are no claw marks in a cougar track. Like a house cat, the cougar keeps its claws inside the paw until it needs them. This track is actual size.

an animal that eats other animals.) Each cat hunts alone and can kill animals five times its own weight. When a mother cougar makes a kill, she brings her kittens to share the feast.

Eastern cougars are endangered because people used to kill them and because humans have changed their habitat.

Powerful leg muscles make a cougar a great leaper. It can jump as high as the roof of a one-story house and as far as half the length of a basketball court.

Bald Eagle

The bald eagle is America's national symbol. Adult bald eagles' heads are covered with white feathers, making them look bald. These feathers don't turn white until the eagles are three years old. Eagles can live to be thirty.

Bald eagles often eat fish. The eagle flies over the water and catches the fish in its sharp claws, which are called talons. Back at its nest, high in a tall tree, the eagle feeds part of the fish to its babies and eats the rest itself. In places where

The bald eagle's voice is a thin, chattering sound that seems weak for such a big bird.

When eagle wings are spread wide, the distance from one wingtip to the other (called the wingspan) can be seven feet—taller than the average man.

Fish are the bald eagle's favorite food.

there are a lot of fish, many bald eagles sometimes gather.

Working together, a pair of eagles will build on to an old nest year after year, making it bigger and bigger. Baby eagles live in the nest for about nine weeks. Then they learn to fly and can go anywhere they want.

Bald eagles are in danger because of pesticide poisoning.

Although bald eagles don't nest in every state, they can be seen in just about every part of America at one time or another as they migrate.

The sharp, curved beak is made for tearing off chunks of meat to eat.

Bald eagles have excellent eyesight for spotting food at long distances.

Hualapai Mexican Vole

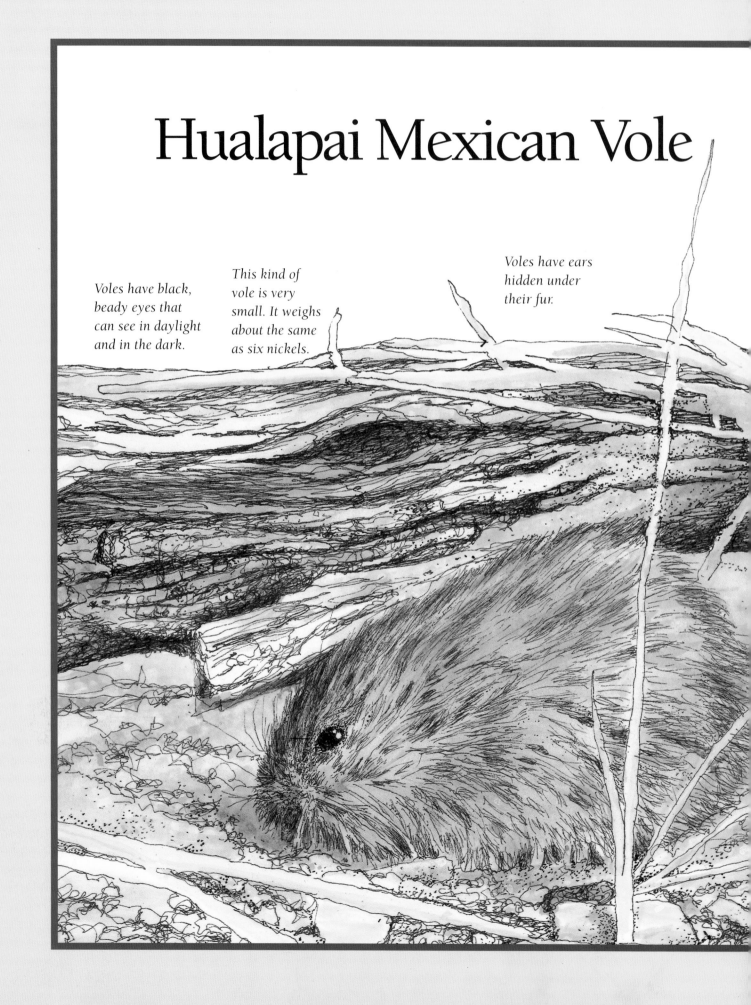

Voles have black, beady eyes that can see in daylight and in the dark.

This kind of vole is very small. It weighs about the same as six nickels.

Voles have ears hidden under their fur.

Voles are similar to mice. One of their habits is neatness, and they spend much time grooming their thick fur.

Voles live in burrows, but they come above ground to eat plants. They make runways in the grass to help them escape predators. Vole predators include hawks, skunks, bobcats, and foxes.

This kind of vole lives only in the Hualapai (pronounced *WAL-a-pie*) Mountains in Arizona. It is very rare, and there probably are only a few of them left alive.

Hualapai Mexican voles are endangered because of habitat loss and because they are isolated from other voles.

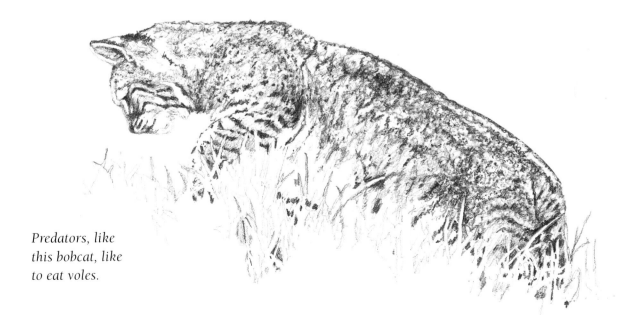

Predators, like this bobcat, like to eat voles.

California Condor

The California condor is one of the world's largest birds. It can measure nine feet from wingtip to wingtip.

This bird is a scavenger, which means it eats dead animals instead of killing them itself. The condor soars high in the sky until its keen eyes spot a meal on the ground—maybe a dead deer or elk. Then it lands and eats.

Female condors do not lay eggs until they are five or six years old, and then they lay only one egg every other year.

Condors watch for smaller scavengers—like crows or eagles—feeding on a dead animal. Then the condor flies there and gets a meal.

The condor's head and neck have few— if any—feathers

The condor can soar for hours without flapping its wings. This way, it can go a long distance looking for food.

Several years ago, biologists captured the few remaining wild condors. They raised the birds in zoos and are now releasing some young condors into the wild.

California condors have no natural enemies, and if they avoid illness and accidents can live to be forty years old. They are endangered because they sometimes get poisoned or accidentally fly into power lines. Also, people used to kill condors.

Woodland Caribou

Woodland caribou are large members of the deer family. They have long antlers and big feet that help them stay on top of the snow instead of sinking. By standing on top of tall snowdrifts, caribou can reach high into trees to get a

Male caribou (called bulls) have large antlers. Every year, the antlers fall off, then grow back in the spring.

Caribou have an excellent sense of smell. This helps them know when predators, like cougars, are nearby.

plant called lichen (pronounced *LI-ken*) to eat.

Woodland caribou spend the winter high in the mountains where few other animals can live.

They are endangered because much of their habitat has been lost.

Long ago, people in some countries tamed wild caribou. When they are tame, caribou are called reindeer.

The owl's ears are hidden beneath its feathers. From high in a tree, an owl can hear a mouse rustling in the grass.

The eyes can see in the daylight and in the dark. They are locked in their sockets—to look sideways, the owl must turn its whole head.

Northern Spotted Owl

The northern spotted owl lives only in forests where trees have been growing for more than one hundred years. It likes old, tall trees because they have many cavities for nesting and few branches near the ground. This makes it easier for the owl to fly around.

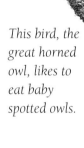

This bird is nocturnal (pronounced *nock-TUR-nal*), which means it is active mostly at night. Its hooting call sounds almost like a barking dog.

The northern spotted owl eats flying squirrels, voles, and mice. The owl perches on a branch, then swoops down quietly and snatches the victim in its talons.

This owl is endangered due to loss of habitat.

This bird, the great horned owl, likes to eat baby spotted owls.

This owl's favorite place—old forests—is disappearing due to logging.

Grizzly Bear

Grizzlies like to live in the wilderness, far away from people. When humans move into grizzly habitat, there can be trouble. Grizzlies are large and strong and can be very dangerous.

In autumn, the grizzly enters a cave or den on the side of a mountain. It stays in its den sleeping until winter has passed.

In spring, the bear awakes very hungry and goes looking for something to eat—like a deer or elk that died during the winter. The grizzly also eats garbage, grass, bugs, and any small animals it can catch.

Grizzlies are endangered because people used to kill them and because their habitat is disappearing.

This is the actual size of a grizzly track. The marks out in front of each toe are from the claws. When standing on its hind legs, a male grizzly can be eight feet tall—a foot taller than basketball star Shaquille O'Neal.

Grizzlies have long, sharp claws, but they don't climb trees very well. However, their powerful legs help them run as fast as horses.

Grizzlies can't see very well and can hear no better than humans, but they can smell food two miles away.

The grizzly has a hump of muscle above its front shoulders that other bears don't have.

Grizzly fur can be black, tan, or brown.

Point Arena Mountain Beaver

This animal is not really a beaver. It doesn't build dams, gnaw through tree trunks, or have a large flat tail.

The mountain beaver lives on cool, moist mountain slopes. It spends its days underground in a tunnel, but comes out at night to eat green plants. It is a good swimmer and doesn't mind when its tunnel gets flooded. It makes a sound like a shrill whistle and will grate its teeth when frightened or angry. Sometimes other animals use tunnels built by mountain beavers.

Mountain beavers exist only in North America, and this kind of mountain beaver lives only near the town of Point Arena in California. It is very rare.

Point Arena mountain beavers are endangered because the small area where they live is being used more and more by humans.

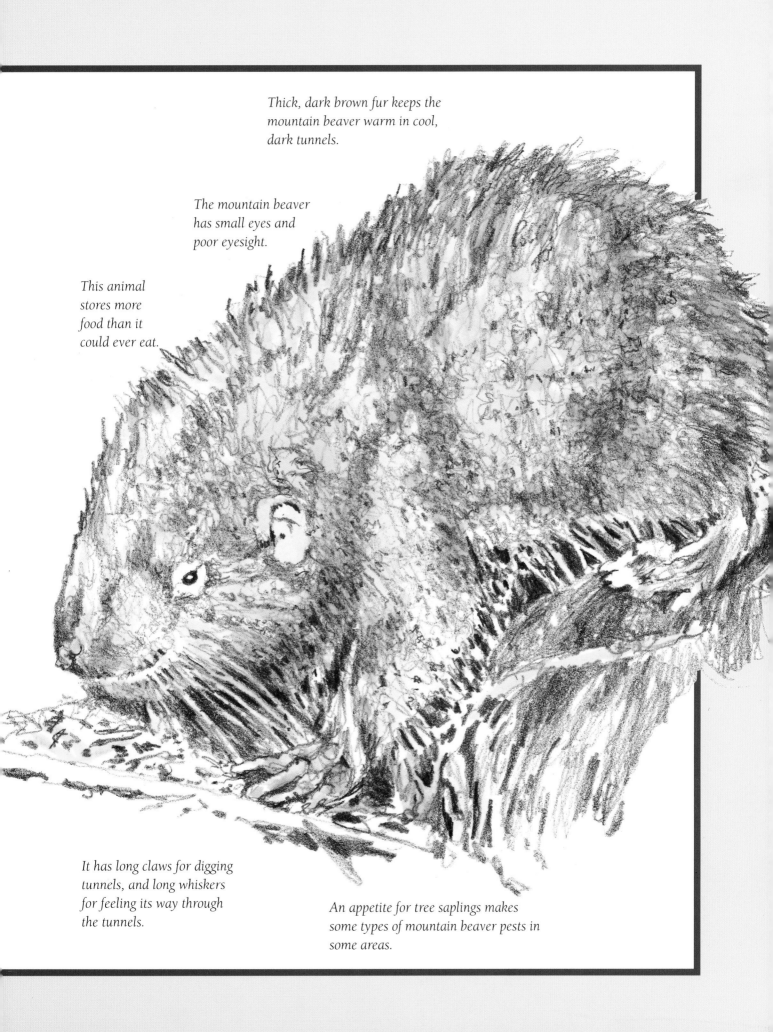

Thick, dark brown fur keeps the mountain beaver warm in cool, dark tunnels.

The mountain beaver has small eyes and poor eyesight.

This animal stores more food than it could ever eat.

It has long claws for digging tunnels, and long whiskers for feeling its way through the tunnels.

An appetite for tree saplings makes some types of mountain beaver pests in some areas.

How You Can Help

Do you care about endangered animals? You can help them, you know. One way to help is to learn more about them. You can read more books and magazine articles and watch television programs about these animals.

Once you learn about endangered animals, tell your friends, parents, and teachers. If lots of people know about these animals, they are more likely to be saved and not become extinct.

You also can write letters about endangered animals. The best people to write to are your senators and representative in Washington, D.C. Tell them you want the endangered animals to be protected. Ask your parents for the names of your senators and representative. The address is easy:

Senator _____ (put the person's name here)
U. S. Senate
Washington, D.C. 20515

OR

Representative _____ (put the person's name here)
U. S. House of Representatives
Washington, D.C. 20515